R0110497344

08/2018

W9-AQV-480

Parents and Caregivers,

Stone Arch Readers are designed to provide enjoyable reading experiences, as well as opportunities to develop vocabulary, literacy skills, and comprehension. Here are a few ways to support your beginning reader:

- Talk with your child about the ideas addressed in the story.

- Discuss each illustration, mentioning the characters, where they are, and what they are doing.

- Read with expression, pointing to each word. You may want to read the whole story through and then revisit parts of the story to ensure that the meanings of words or phrases are understood.

- Talk about why the character did what he or she did and what your child would do in that situation.

- Help your child connect with characters and events in the story.

Remember, reading with your child should be fun, not forced. Each moment spent reading with your child is a priceless investment in his or her literacy life.

Gail Saunders-Smith, Ph.D.

STONE ARCH READERS
are published by Stone Arch Books, a Capstone Imprint
1710 Roe Crest Drive
North Mankato, Minnesota 56003
www.capstonepub.com

Library of Congress Cataloging-in-Publication Data
Klein, Adria F. (Adria Fay), 1947-
Big train / by Adria Klein ; illustrated by Craig Cameron.
p. cm. -- (Stone Arch readers: Train time)
Summary: Engine is looking for Passenger Car
and all his other car friends.
ISBN 978-1-4342-4191-7 (library binding)
ISBN 978-1-4342-4886-2 (pbk.)
1. Locomotives--Juvenile fiction. 2. Railroad trains--Juvenile
fiction. [1. Locomotives--Fiction. 2. Railroad trains--Fiction.]
I. Cameron, Craig, ill. II. Title.
PZ7.K678324Big 2013
[E]--dc23
2012026291

Reading Consultants:
Gail Saunders-Smith, Ph.D.
Melinda Melton Crow, M.Ed.
Laurie K. Holland, Media Specialist
Designer: Russell Griesmer

Printed in China.
122015   009349R

Big Train

written by
Adria F. Klein

illustrated by
Craig Cameron

STONE ARCH BOOKS
a capstone imprint

Engine was a little train.
He was all alone.

"Where are my friends?"
he said.

Engine saw one friend.

He was hiding.

"Hi, Engine," he said.

Engine saw another friend.

He was hiding.

"Hi, Engine," he said.

Engine saw another friend.

He was hiding.

"Hi, Engine," he said.

"Look at all my friends!"
Engine said.

"Now I am a big train!"
he said.

Toot! Toot!

STORY WORDS

engine   alone   hiding

train   friends

Word Count: 65

STONE ARCH READERS
LEVEL 1
Circus Train
written by
Adria F. Klein
Illustrated by
Craig Cameron

STONE ARCH READERS
LEVEL 1
City Train
written by
Adria F. Klein
Illustrated by
Craig Cameron

STONE ARCH READERS
LEVEL 1
Freight Train
written by
Adria F. Klein
Illustrated by
Craig Cameron